P

PIG IN THE CITY

The Big City Adventure

The Big City Adventure

Adapted by Neil Morris
from the junior novelization by
Justine Korman and Ron Fontes
based on the motion picture screenplay
written by George Miller Judy Morris Mark Lamprell
based on characters created by Dick King-Smith

PUFFIN BOOKS

PUFFIN BOOKS

Published by the Penguin Group
Penguin Books Ltd, 27 Wrights Lane, London W8 5TZ, England
Penguin Putnam Inc., 375 Hudson Street, New York, New York 10014, USA
Penguin Books Australia Ltd, Ringwood, Victoria, Australia
Penguin Books Canada Ltd, 10 Alcorn Avenue, Toronto, Ontario, Canada M4V 3B2
Penguin Books (NZ) Ltd, Private Bag 102902, NSMC, Auckland, New Zealand

Penguin Books Ltd, Registered Offices: Harmondsworth, Middlesex, England

First published 1998
1 3 5 7 9 10 8 6 4 2

Puffin Film and TV Tie-in edition first published 1998

Set in 15/20 Berkeley

Printed and bound in Great Britain by Ladybird

British Library Cataloguing in Publication Data
A CIP catalogue record for this book is available from the British Library

ISBN 0–141–30246–1

Chapter One

If only . . .

Remember the story of Babe, the polite little pig who turned out to be a farmer's best friend? That's right, the pig who astonished the farming world by winning the National Sheepdog Trials. No sheepdog had ever got a perfect score at the Trials, but this amazing sheep-pig did!

When Babe went back to the farm with his master, Farmer Hoggett, he was famous. All the villagers cheered, and the animals made a fuss too. Sheep trotted down from the hills to welcome him home. 'Babe! Ba-a-be! Ba-a-a-be!' they bleated.

By the time he reached Hoggett Farm, Babe's heart was filled with pride. Mrs Hoggett bustled out to meet her husband and his remarkable pig. Of course Mr Hoggett was delighted that Babe was Grand Champion, but he was just as pleased to be back on his farm. He was a quiet man, and he found his greatest pleasure in honest work.

So, the next day, Farmer Hoggett was back at work, fitting a new water-pump to the well. He put the pump on a wooden platform and climbed down into the well. At this point Babe's new-found fame went to his head. Without being asked, he decided to help. If only he hadn't . . .

As Hoggett lowered the heavy pump, Babe

leant over the edge of the well. If only he hadn't . . .

A block of stone gave way under Babe's trotters, and he fell down the well. When he landed on the platform, it shot straight down and hit Hoggett on the head. 'Boss!' Babe squealed, his little voice echoing in the well.

If only he hadn't interfered . . .

Next day the farmhouse looked more like a hospital. Farmer Hoggett lay in bed, wrapped in bandages and plaster casts. When Babe crept

up to sit next to his master, Mrs Hoggett frowned at him. The farmer slowly raised his bandaged hand and scratched the pig's head. 'S-sorry, boss,' Babe whispered.

Mrs Hoggett went off to shear the sheep. She

would have to do everything while her husband was laid up. But the sheep were not at all happy with her clumsy clipping. 'Sa-a-ave us!' they bleated.

Just then two men came striding across the farmyard. Mrs Hoggett's heart sank. Briefcases, suits – the men were from the bank! And that could mean only one thing. She hurried back to the farmhouse and rifled through a pile of papers. At last she found the important letter. It said, 'Grand fair . . . guest appearance . . . pig

. . . sheep-herding demonstration . . . plane tickets . . . generous fee.'

'Jumping jam 'n' jellies,' cried Mrs Hoggett, 'we might just do it!' By *it* she meant go to the fair, earn the fee and pay the men from the bank so they could keep the farm. Farmer Hoggett agreed. After all, if a pig could become a champion sheepdog, anything was possible.

Mrs Hoggett called out for Babe, but there was no reply. Fly and Rex, the sheepdogs, knew where the pig was hiding and ran off to the barn to get him. Babe was determined not to go. But then he heard his master's gentle voice. 'Come, pig,' Hoggett said.

Now Babe was in two minds. He didn't want to leave the farm – and especially Fly, who looked after him like a mother. And Ferdinand the duck, his best friend, had begged him to stay. But Babe didn't want to let his master down.

At last the little pig trotted out of the barn. Mrs Hoggett swept him up in her arms and

carried him to the truck. Then she blew her husband a kiss. 'Don't worry, heart,' she shouted, 'I'll guard him with my life.'

And so Babe went off into the big wide world. This time the sheep bleated, 'Save the farm, Babe! Sa-a-ve the fa-a-a-rm!' Ferdinand agreed, as he tried desperately to keep up.

As the truck drove away, the men from the bank put up a sign that read, 'Farm for Sale'. Only Babe could save the farm now.

Chapter Two
Scram!

Mrs Hoggett sat patiently in the jumbo jet, waiting for take-off. Down in the plane's hold, Babe tried to be brave as the engines roared into life and rattled his cage.

Ferdinand, the desperate duck, arrived just in time. But as the jumbo took off, it left him flapping far behind. He had never seen such a huge featherless flying machine before, and he asked a passing flock of geese if they knew where it was heading. 'Just follow us,' the geese replied.

When the plane landed, Babe's cage was taken by conveyor belt to a big room full of luggage. There a beagle was sniffing his way through a mountain of suitcases. The words 'Drug Detection' were printed on the dog's jacket.

'Excuse me,' Babe said politely, 'but I seem to have lost my human.'

'Look, pal, I'm busy,' the dog yapped. 'I've got to sniff all this stuff. Sniff, sniff, sniff. I'm a sniffer dog, see?' The beagle lifted his big, wet nose. 'It's all in the hooter, the schnoz, the smelling instrument.' Then the dog showed the pig what happened when he sniffed out something interesting. He jumped up and down, barking as loudly as he could.

Customs officers came running in at once. They grabbed the case next to the beagle and looked on their list to find out who its owner was. It was Mrs Hoggett! The farmer's wife and Babe were marched off to be questioned.

While the officers shuffled their papers, Mrs Hoggett began to lose her patience. 'Chop-chop,' she cried. 'If we miss our connecting flight, we won't make the shuttle. And if we miss the shuttle, we won't arrive in time for the fair. And if we miss the fair, we won't earn the money. And if we don't have the money, the bank won't take "sorry, we missed the flight" for an answer!'

At last Mrs Hoggett and Babe were released, but too late to catch their connecting flight. Even worse, there was no flight home for days. They were stranded at the airport. Mrs Hoggett tried phoning hotels, but none took pets – and they certainly didn't want a pig.

Things got even worse when a security guard turned them out of the airport. 'Scram!' he shouted when he saw Babe. 'This isn't a farm.'

Outside, the farmer's wife had a real shock. Car horns honked, brakes squealed and exhaust fumes filled the air. Where could they possibly go? Luckily an airport cleaner took pity on them and slipped Mrs Hoggett a piece of paper. The address on it read, 'Flealands Hotel, 349 Random Canal'.

They set off at once. Coming from the peace and quiet of Hoggett Hollow, they were amazed at the sights, the sounds and the speed of the city. They walked along wide streets until they came to a maze of narrow alleys, canals and

bridges. At last Mrs Hoggett found what she was looking for. The sign on a big, ramshackle building read: 'Flealands Hotel'.

Chapter Three

Are you crazy?

When Mrs Hoggett knocked on the door of the hotel, it was flung open at once. 'I'd like a room for myself and a pig, please,' she said.

'Are you crazy?' the landlady cried. 'Animals in here? What kind of establishment do you think this is? Am I aware of the city regulations? Yes! Do I want to break the law? Definitely not!' And with that she slammed the door.

Mrs Hoggett was disappointed. But as she and Babe trudged off, they heard a voice whispering, 'Pssst!' It was the landlady, who pulled them into an alley next to the hotel. 'Will an attic room do?' she asked brightly.

'Of course,' Mrs Hoggett replied. 'But I thought you said . . .'

'Oh, that was just for the neighbours,' the landlady laughed, leading them up a rickety staircase. 'Do we provide meals? No. But is there a shop near by? Yes, two streets away. And what is the golden rule? Never answer the front door. Why? Because it might be an inspector.'

On the way up the stairs, Babe saw eyes peering out at them from various rooms. Three dogs watched as they went past – Nigel the bulldog, Alan the mastiff and Flealick, a little dog whose lame back legs were mounted on

wheels. Flealick tried to follow them, but his wheels got stuck on the stairs.

When they reached the top floor, the landlady showed them into their room. 'Where's the payphone?' she recited. 'In the hall, but for local calls only. Where does the little piggy stay at all times? In the room!'

Mrs Hoggett put a photo of her husband on the bedside table, and then went off to find a long-distance phone. Babe jumped on to a chair and looked out of the window. The city stretched as far as he could see. It was full of skyscrapers, towers and chimneys, and the little pig wondered when he would see his first city sheep. But just then the door opened and a tiny monkey scampered in.

Before Babe could do anything, the monkey picked up Mrs Hoggett's suitcase and ran off with it. Babe chased the monkey down the stairs, but the thief suddenly dashed into a room and slammed the door shut. The pig banged on the door as hard as he could.

Babe could only stare when the door was opened by a chimpanzee in a pretty dress. Behind her, Babe could see two other chimps watching TV. And behind them all was the tiny monkey. But when Babe asked for the suitcase back, the chimps just ignored him.

The little pig decided to take a firm line, like a sheepdog with sheep. 'I must warn you,' he said seriously, 'I can be ferocious when provoked.' He was surprised to see a look of shock on the chimps' faces, but then he heard a very deep voice behind him.

'And what have we here?' boomed the voice, and Babe was astonished to find that it belonged to an enormous orang-utan dressed as a butler. Babe explained about the suitcase, but, before he could finish, another strange character stepped into the room. This time it was a man dressed in an old clown's costume. As he stared at Babe, they both heard the landlady's voice.

'Uncle Fugly!' the landlady cried. The clown hastily picked Babe up and hid him in a trunk. The landlady came in with Mrs Hoggett and introduced her to the clown, whose name was Fugly Floom. 'I'm afraid there's been a theft upstairs, Uncle,' the landlady said. 'Mrs Hoggett has lost her pig.'

Floom waved his arms about in strange gestures, which his niece somehow understood. 'He saw what looked like a pig leaving this establishment,' the landlady interpreted. 'Where did it go? Towards the beach.'

Chapter Four
Total chaos

Mrs Hoggett searched the crowded promenade. 'Pig!' she cried. 'PIG!'

Two policemen on motorcycles thought she was referring to them and set off after her. Totally unaware of this, the farmer's wife turned into a back alley, only to find herself facing a gang of dancing rollerbladers.

'Hey, what've you got in the bag?' their leader asked.

Mrs Hoggett froze, suddenly aware of the danger. Then she made a run for it. The young man grabbed her handbag, but she hung on and dragged him along on his blades. When she reached the end of the alley, she swung him right into the path of the police motorbikes. There was a tremendous crash and wheels flew everywhere.

At that moment a skateboarder swerved into a ladder, knocking down a workman who was sticking up a poster. Mrs Hoggett was soon covered in wet, sticky glue. To make things worse, a policeman came marching up to her and flipped open his notebook.

Meanwhile, Babe was having lots of excitement too. Having sent Mrs Hoggett away, Fugly Floom and his orang-utan butler, Thelonius, took the little pig to their latest performance, in a children's hospital. First the clown pretended to saw Babe in half. Next his magic made it look as if the pig's head was on a silver plate. But then things went horribly wrong.

The clown was just about to light a pretend

cannon when he tripped over Babe. Floom's match lit the stage curtains instead, and this set off the fire alarm and the water sprinklers. There was total chaos, and the young audience laughed their heads off as a soaking clown, pig, orang-utan and chimps scattered in all directions.

Chapter Five

Fortune favours the brave

Babe's stomach was rumbling. For an hour he had been sitting in Fugly Floom's kitchen while the clown ate and drank everything in sight. When at last he could eat no more, Thelonius led his master into the living-room to rest. The orang-utan lifted the clown's feet on to a stool and tucked a blanket round his shoulders.

The youngest chimp, whose name was Easy, rolled a peanut-butter jar towards Babe. The jar was almost empty, but it was better than nothing to the starving pig.

'Hey, we look after our own first,' said Easy's brother, Bob.

'Yeah, listen to your big brother,' added Zootie, Bob's wife. 'Because he's, you know, your big brother!'

Babe didn't hear any of this. He was too busy trying to reach the bottom of the jar with his tongue. But he just couldn't get at the peanut butter. Then he found to his horror that his snout was stuck.

Thelonius took pity on Babe and pulled the jar off his snout. But Babe was angry as well as hungry. 'Where's my reward?' he asked the orang-utan. 'That clown promised me a reward for my performance. My human will be back soon, so I'd better get my reward *now*!'

Thelonius hated to hear any criticism of his master, so he quickly rammed the jar back on Babe's snout.

'I know where your reward is,' Bob whispered to the pig.

'Oo do?' asked Babe, his voice muffled by the jar.

'Oodle-doodles of reward,' Bob promised, pointing to a trapdoor in the ceiling.

The other chimps tried not to laugh as they helped Bob build a tower of old newspapers, boxes and other junk. 'I'd go up myself, only I'm collapsophobic,' Bob explained, as the others sniggered.

Babe looked up at the trap and remembered what Fly the sheepdog had told him. 'Fortune favours the brave,' the little pig said. 'Right?'

The chimps nodded eagerly, and Babe started the difficult climb. At first he did well, but soon the tower of junk was swaying like a tall tree. Babe clambered on up.

'Just don't look down,' Easy shouted. So what did Babe do? He looked down! In his mind he found himself back at the farm, looking over the edge of the well at Farmer Hoggett. The little pig closed his eyes, just as Bob gave the tower a shove. Babe squealed as he fell from the toppling tower, straight through an open window.

The plucky pig managed to cling to an awning outside the window. But his trotters soon slipped and, with a loud splash, he plunged into the canal below. Unfortunately this was not nice, clean country water. It was nasty, filthy city water. Babe doggy-paddled to the bank as fast as he could.

Tug, the thieving little monkey, let Babe back into Flealands Hotel. But when he got up to Fugly Floom's room, the chimpanzees were arguing with the orang-utan and scarcely noticed the shivering pig.

As always, Thelonius was defending the clown. 'He taught us to walk upright and put the clothes on our backs,' said the orang-utan.

'But he didn't give me my reward!' Babe insisted.

At that Thelonius went mad. He grabbed Babe in his long arms and flung him out of the window. With an even louder splash, the pig found himself back in the canal.

When at last he got back to his own attic room, tired and dripping wet, Babe stared out

of the window at the busy city. As night fell, the skyscrapers twinkled like giant fairy castles. Babe wondered where Mrs Hoggett could be. It was tough being a pig alone in the city. He tried to remember some of the important things that the sheepdogs had taught him, but the past and the farm seemed so far away, like a half-forgotten dream. Slowly, sadly, Babe fell asleep.

Next morning he was woken by a commotion on the hotel stairs. He went out to the landing and saw two ambulance men carrying Fugly Floom out on a stretcher. The landlady was holding her uncle's hand, and she looked very worried. Young Easy was trying to console Thelonius. 'He'll be back,' Easy said gently. 'The clown always comes back.'

In another part of the city, a new arrival was trying to get his breath back after the most tiring flight of his life. It was Ferdinand, the demented duck, who was resting in the arms of a stone angel on top of a church. He was exhausted, but he was still determined. 'Pig . . . p-pig . . .' Ferdinand called weakly.

Chapter Six
The chase is on

By that evening, Babe was absolutely starving. He politely asked Nigel, Alan and Flealick if they had any food, but the dogs' answer was no. The chimps said the same, but Babe was pleased when Bob decided to go out and do something about it. His wife Zootie was alarmed at the idea of him being out without a human, but Bob was determined.

Babe followed the chimps along the dark, shadowy streets. Bob was unhappy at being lumbered with a pig, but Babe insisted he would do anything to help.

'Oh yeah,' jeered Easy. 'What can *you* do?'

Babe thought for a moment. 'I can herd sheep!' he said.

The chimps chuckled, but then Bob had an

idea. He led them to a shop two streets away from the hotel. At the back was a big wire fence. 'There are sheep in there,' Bob told Babe, holding open a hole in the fence.

'What kind?' Babe asked. 'Border Leicester or Scottish Blackface?'

'Bull terrier and Dobermann pinscher,' Bob replied. 'Very exotic breeds.'

Babe had never heard of those, but Rex the sheepdog had told him always to do his best. 'Where do you want me to herd them?' he asked Bob.

'That's up to you,' the chimp answered. 'Just keep them occupied till we've got the necessaries.'

Babe wriggled through the fence and called politely, 'Hello, anybody home?' The answer was a loud, spine-chilling snarl. 'Um . . . anybody else?' asked Babe.

A huge, menacing Dobermann dog lumbered out of the shadows. And before Babe could turn and run, a growling bull terrier came charging straight at him! Fortunately for the pig, both dogs were chained to a stake in the ground and their jaws couldn't reach him.

'I was only trying to be civil,' said Babe, as he

went back through the fence. This was a mistake, for it annoyed the bull terrier so much that he yanked the stake right out of the ground.

The chase was on! Babe squealed around the street corner, while the dogs caught their chain on a lamp-post. The pig ran into an alley and found himself in a maze of old cardboard boxes, where homeless cats and dogs lived. They looked on in amazement as he disappeared into the nearby scrapyard.

The dogs followed, but they lost Babe in all

the junk and ended up facing each other. All they could hear was the sound of their own panting. 'Stop breathing!' the bull terrier ordered. Both dogs held their breath, but they could still hear panting. They looked up and saw Babe perched on a box just above their heads. The chase was on again!

Junk flew everywhere as the dogs hunted Babe all over the scrapyard. Piles of tin cans collapsed, hundreds of old tyres rolled, and still Babe managed to keep his trotters ahead. The bull terrier got so annoyed that he finally turned on the Dobermann.

'Wait, I'm your only pal!' the Dobermann protested. But the bull terrier just ground his mighty teeth. The Dobermann could see that his former friend was beyond reason, so he ran for it.

Meanwhile Babe was trying to get as far away as possible. The chimps had now left the shop and were munching jellybeans and chocolates as they watched the chase with interest. They wondered if they should lend Babe a helping hand, but decided against it. 'Why get involved?' Easy shrugged.

The bull terrier had caught a rusty old lawnmower on the end of his chain, but it didn't seem to slow him down. He finally caught up with Babe by the canal bridge in front of Flealands Hotel. Babe knew the game was up. He turned to face his attacker, snout to nose.

The bull terrier lunged, but luckily the mad dog's sharp teeth cut through Babe's collar rather than cutting his throat. Once again Babe went with a splash into the canal.

Without a moment's hesitation, the bull terrier launched himself after Babe, but this time there was no splash. The lawnmower got caught on the bridge, and the dog found himself dangling from his chain, just above the murky canal. He strained as hard as he could, which only made the chain slip and slowly lower him, head first, into the water. His bark soon turned to a gurgle.

Chimps and dogs watched from the hotel, and the homeless animals crept along to see the bull terrier's struggle. Suddenly they all heard a splash. It was Babe, doggy-paddling towards a boat on the canal.

Babe managed to free the boat and push it under the bull terrier. The dog suddenly gasped for air, but he was still held by the chain. Babe shouted for help, but none of the bystanders moved. Then Tug, the tiny monkey, climbed down the chain and unhooked it from the dog's collar.

Babe made for the canal bank and collapsed, exhausted. He was soon surrounded by homeless animals, all keen to get to know him. Babe was a hero once more!

The starving creatures all began to ask their new hero for food and shelter, but how could he help them? Then Babe saw Bob and the other chimps standing in front of the hotel munching jellybeans, and he had an idea. 'If we all went inside and lined up, I'm sure there'd be enough to go round,' he said.

Bob was horrified. 'You're talking as if you're the word around here,' he sneered.

'I'd say he is,' said a low, growling voice. It was the bull terrier. 'Whatever the pig says goes. Anyone disagree?'

No one dared challenge those powerful jaws. 'Fine by me,' Bob squeaked.

As the homeless animals filed into Flealands Hotel, the bull terrier handed Babe his spiked leather collar. 'Pig, it would honour me if you would wear this,' the dog said.

The animals formed an orderly queue inside the hotel, as one by one Tug handed them a ration of jellybeans. The bull terrier insisted that everyone thank Babe for the food. Bob didn't want to but, when the bull terrier growled at him, he whispered, 'Thanks.'

'Don't mention it,' Babe replied politely.

Chapter Seven
Raided

The animals at Flealands Hotel were still hungry, but they were a lot happier than usual. And there was something else to celebrate. Zootie had not only had a baby – she was the happy mother of twins! Bob was a very proud father, and Easy was a delighted uncle. Babe

started singing, to celebrate the baby chimps' birth. The other animals joined in the squealing, howling song.

Their voices carried over the canal, between the rows of skyscrapers, all the way to a stone angel on top of a church. Ferdinand lifted his head and listened. There was something about that sound . . . yes, it was Babe, his lucky pig! The desperate duck flew off at once in search of the singer.

Unfortunately, Ferdinand was not the only one who heard the wailing, squealing and howling. One of the Flealands' neighbours was particularly horrified. 'The place must be teeming with nasty animals!' she shrieked, picking up the phone to ring the police.

Ferdinand followed the noise to the hotel, and tapped his beak on the window. Babe couldn't believe his eyes and rushed to let the duck in. Ferdinand was surprised to see Babe wearing a spiked collar. 'You look . . . different,' the duck said.

'Yeah, well, this place takes it out of you,' Babe sighed. So much had happened since they left the farm!

Just then there was a loud crash, as a gloved hand smashed through the glass panel of the front door. In seconds, the hotel was stormed by a gang of uniformed police raiders.

The raiders set to work grabbing cats and dogs and taking them to a van waiting outside. Ferdinand panicked and tried to take off, but a leather-clad cop grabbed him by the neck. 'Hey, supper!' the cop chuckled. But he soon let go when the bull terrier charged at him.

A huge, padded man leapt on the bull terrier, forced a metal muzzle over his jaws and dragged him away. Others shot tranquillizer darts at the chimpanzees. Zootie begged Thelonius to help them, but the orang-utan

just turned to Babe and said, 'You did this!'
Then a gang of policemen threw a net over the
orang-utan and hauled him away too.

Babe stood there, wondering what to do,
when the collar of a lead dropped over his
head. Just as the pig was being taken away,
Ferdinand flew straight into a raider, who
bumped into a bookcase – thud! – which fell
on to a table – thump! – which knocked over a
vase – crash! – and in all the confusion Babe
broke free, dragging the lead behind him.

Outside, the raiders were throwing the three dog friends, Nigel, Alan and little Flealick, into a van. But the driver said, 'This one's useless!' and flung Flealick out again. The lame dog refused to be parted from his friends and he snapped at the long white coat of one of the female raiders. Just then the van drove off, dragging Flealick along on his squeaky little wheels.

Babe and Tug, the tiny monkey, ran after the van. At a sharp bend, Flealick was thrown off and he bounced, head over wheels, across the street. The little dog was a bit shaken but otherwise was all right.

'Don't worry,' Flealick barked when Babe and Tug arrived. 'I got their scent. They went this-a-way.' He pointed his nose back towards the hotel.

Babe took a big sniff. 'Actually, Flealick,' he said, 'I think it's that way.'

Ferdinand flew down and flapped his wings. 'What are you doing?' he squawked.

Babe said proudly, 'It's all in the hooter, Ferdie, the schnoz.'

'The what?' the duck screamed.

'The smelling instrument!' Babe explained calmly.

Ferdinand couldn't believe it. 'Let's face it, you're just a little pig in the big city,' he fumed. 'What can you do now? Let's go home.'

Babe wondered whether the duck was right. When he turned, he saw Flealick rolling down the street to save his friends. Babe asked Tug to help him take off the collar. Then he trotted after Flealick.

Ferdinand sighed as he followed his friend.

Chapter Eight

What a surprise!

Babe wondered what had happened to Mrs Hoggett, and the answer was – a lot! You remember that the farmer's wife was searching for Babe when she had a slight accident involving rollerblades, glue and, unfortunately, the police. Well, she ended up covered in glue from head to foot and, even worse, she was arrested by the police.

When she appeared in court, Mrs Hoggett was determined to set the record straight. 'Sir, I used to dismiss pigs,' she told the judge solemnly. 'Then a pig became my husband's best friend, and I must confess that made me jealous. But not any more. What am I if I can't

look after a helpless creature that trusts me? The minute I'm free, I shall continue my search for the pig.'

The judge was moved by Mrs Hoggett's sincere words – and besides, he'd grown up on a farm himself. He let her go free at once.

Mrs Hoggett rushed back to Flealands Hotel, and when she got there she had a terrible shock. The place had been wrecked! Broken glass was everywhere and there was no sign of Babe. Then Mrs Hoggett saw the landlady, slumped in a chair and looking very upset.

'This used to be such a lovely neighbourhood,' the landlady said sadly. 'I wanted to make a kind place where the animals would be OK, and look what's happened. I was away just one night, with my Uncle Fugly on his deathbed. And now poor Fugly's gone for ever. It's all *her* fault!'

The landlady meant the neighbour who had complained about the animals, and Mrs Hoggett decided to deal with this person at

once. But she hadn't noticed that her gluey
dress had hardened and so, when she tried to
rush off, the dress split and snapped in pieces.
'Right!' said Mrs Hoggett. 'Clothes! Got
anything that will fit me?'

Minutes later, Mrs Hoggett came charging
out of the hotel dressed in Fugly Floom's
clown's costume. Imagine the animal-hating
neighbour's surprise when she opened the

door to the farmer's wife dressed as a clown! Mrs Hoggett screamed, 'We want our animals!'

Meanwhile, Babe was also trying to find the animals. If you remember, he had been delighted to find that his snout was a sensitive smelling instrument, so he used it to track the raiders through the city. Ferdinand, Tug and Flealick scurried along behind.

At last Babe's snout told him that they had arrived. They turned the next corner and, sure enough, there was the raiders' van. It was

parked outside a large building with a sign that read, 'University Hospital: Research Laboratory'.

Babe sent Tug up a drainpipe to take a look inside the building. The tiny monkey was shocked to see the chimps and dogs in cages, and Thelonius without his butler's uniform. Tug made wild signals to Babe that their friends were locked up inside.

Babe and the others crept through a side door, and the animals were delighted to see them. Babe had to tell them firmly to keep quiet. Flealick was watching the stairs and he warned that a man in a white coat was coming into the building. Fortunately the lab assistant just yawned and locked the door before going away again.

Now how would they get out? Babe had an idea. They could build a tower up to the ceiling trapdoor, just like the one in the hotel – only better! They freed the animals and used the empty cages to build the tower. Of course,

Thelonius insisted on getting dressed first.

After climbing the tower, the animals had to cross an air-conditioning pipe that connected the research lab to the rest of the hospital. Nigel the bulldog found this very difficult. 'I'm rigid with anxiety,' he woofed. 'I can't do it, can I, Alan?'

For once in his life the bulldog's mastiff friend disagreed with him. 'Yes you can, Nigel!' Alan replied firmly. And Nigel did.

Only one little boy was awake when the

animals crept through the children's ward of the hospital. He thought he was dreaming when he saw the amazing parade: a pig, a duck, some chimps, dogs and cats, and an orang-utan dressed as a butler.

If he had looked out of the window at that moment, the boy would have seen another amazing sight. Mrs Hoggett and the landlady were arriving on Uncle Fugly's old trick tandem. As the bike's wheels turned, the two riders bounced up and down like a see-saw!

The two ladies jumped off the tandem and

looked around. Outside the main hospital building they saw luxurious limousines arriving, bringing women in glittering gowns and men in top hats. Just then a little lame dog rolled out of the shadows, barking frantically.

Mrs Hoggett and the landlady followed Flealick into the nearest building. They found themselves in the hospital kitchen, and they were just about to ask the chef if he had seen any animals, when the kitchen lift opened . . . and there they were! The chef dropped a load of pots and pans when he saw the parade of a pig, a duck, some chimps . . . and all the rest.

The loud crash made the animals run for it, and Mrs Hoggett tried to follow them. But the chef grabbed the braces holding up her clown's trousers, and they stretched and stretched as she kept running. 'Pig! Pig!' cried Mrs Hoggett.

Babe looked back and saw an astonishing sight: the boss's wife was running towards him in a bright clown's costume! Then she shot backwards, as the braces pulled her back into the kitchen. The door slammed shut and the vision was gone.

Babe turned around again, to find that they had run straight into a banqueting hall full of rich guests in evening dress. Little did they know that they had barged in on the hospital's annual fund-raising dinner. The room fell quiet as the guests stared at the animals.

On stage, a woman smothered in jewels was about to make a speech. Hoping the animals were part of the entertainment, she said, 'Oh, what a surprise! I adore surprises.'

But when waiters tried to shoo the animals back into the kitchen, they went in all directions: under the tables, up the pillars, everywhere. 'Please, try to stay calm,' the bejewelled lady begged. Then Tug jumped up on stage and she screamed.

Pandemonium broke out. Mrs Hoggett rushed on to the balcony above the hall and saw that the chef had captured Babe. She grabbed a sash hanging from a crystal chandelier and tied it to her braces. Looking down at the crowd, she cried, 'I am Esme

Cordelia Hoggett, and I've come for my husband's pig!'

Then she launched herself at the chef. The farmer's wife had certainly never bungee-jumped before, but she managed to crash into the chef, and Babe was thrown free . . . right into a stack of cream cakes.

Security guards arrived and tried to catch Babe. But the team made up of a determined farmer's wife, a stubborn landlady, a swinging

orang-utan, a demented duck and many other energetic animals easily won the day. Thousands of balloons floated down from the ceiling as animals and guests laughed and cheered.

Now that the animals were free again, Mrs Hoggett knew only one place where they would all be safe and secure. The city dwellers soon found themselves breathing fresh country air when they moved to Hoggett Hollow.

The landlady rented out Flealands Hotel, and the money helped to save Hoggett Farm. Mrs Hoggett had found a friend for life in Thelonius. The orang-utan thought of the farmer's wife as his new boss, even though she went back to wearing her ordinary clothes.

For Babe and his master, things soon got back to normal. Farmer Hoggett took his pig out to the well and turned the tap on. There was a gurgle, then a splutter, and finally a spurt of clear water from the shiny spout.

Hoggett turned to Babe. 'That'll do, Pig,' he said gently. 'That'll do.'